JATAKA TALES SERIES

Golden Foot

Inspired by Nazli Gellek
Adapted by Karen Stone
Illustrated by Rosalyn White

DHARMA PUBLISHING

Copyright © 1976 by Dharma Publishing. All rights reserved.
Printed in the United States of America by Dharma Press,
5856 Doyle St., Emeryville, California.
Endpapers by Margie Horton.

nce upon a time, long ago in ancient
India, the Buddha was born as a Royal
Stag. He was a creature of grace and beauty
with a coat the color of pure gold. His horns
rose above his head like a silver wreath
and his eyes sparkled like round jewels.
So brightly did his hooves sparkle in the
sunlight that he was called Golden Foot.

Many hundreds of gentle, spotted deer
followed after the Stag, honoring him as
their king, and the king chose a graceful
young doe to be his queen. Living peacefully
together in a great pine forest, they had no
fear of danger.

Early one morning before the sun arose, a clever hunter came to the forest to lay a trap. With a rope, he made a noose that he hid among the pines along the grassy path. At the end of this path was a cool fresh spring where the herd came to drink when they were thirsty.

That day, the Royal Stag came down the
path alone while the doe and the other deer
followed behind him. As he approached the
stream, he caught his foot in the hidden
snare and could not free himself.

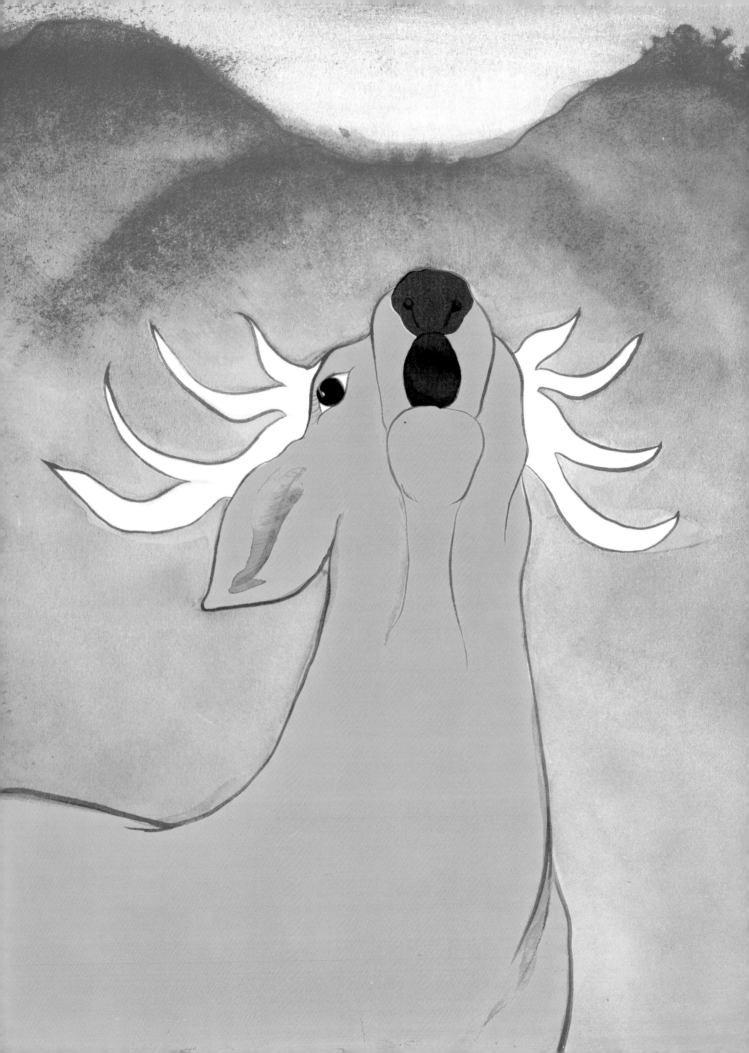

Golden Foot pulled this way and that, but the more he struggled, the tighter the noose became until he cried out in pain. Hearing his cries, the herd panicked and fled. The doe searched for her mate, but nowhere was he to be seen. Quickly she ran back along the grassy path to the stream, and there she found the Stag, weary and sad.

"Golden Foot, you are stronger than you think. Try to use all your strength to break your bonds!"

Yet, try as he might, the trap held fast. Seeing
that his struggle seemed hopeless, the doe thought to
herself, "All the many gentle deer will not be able to
live without their leader to guide them."

And she comforted the stag, saying, "Don't be afraid, I shall stay close by, and when your captor comes, I shall plead for your freedom."

It was not long before they heard the hunter crashing through the brush. He appeared carrying a huge sword in one hand and a sharp-pointed knife in the other. His burning eyes told of the treachery in his heart. Slowly, the doe went forward to meet him.

Standing at a respectful distance, she greeted him saying, "My mate is the Golden Stag, wise beyond compare. Spare the life of the King of Deer and take my own as fair exchange."

Hearing her speak, the hunter was dumbfounded. "Even human beings do not give up their lives for their king. What can this mean?"

Gazing at the doe, his heart was moved, and he thought, "This graceful creature speaks sweetly in the language of men. She has won my heart. Today, I will grant life to her and the Royal Stag." And in the spirit of kindness, he set the Stag free.

Whereupon the king of Deer thought, "This hunter has spared us and all the many hundreds of deer who would other wise have no leader. I must give him a proper gift in return."

Going to the foot of a tree nearby, Golden Foot sharply struck the ground with his pointed hoof and unearthed three shining, magic jewels.

These he gave to the hunter, saying, "My friend, with these three wish-fulfilling gems, you and your family will be protected. So never again take the life of any creature, and wherever you go, offer your help to those in need."

And reminding the hunter to heed these words, the Stag and the doe disappeared into the forest.

After telling this tale, the Buddha said, "A long time ago, Channa, our brother who is not yet kind to others, was the hunter. This gentle woman who taught her husband the virtue of kindness was the faithful doe, and I was Golden Foot, the Royal Stag.

Shakyamuni Buddha told his disciples many stories of his previous lives as a compassionate Bodhisattva. These ancient, symbolic legends, called the *Jataka Tales*, may be understood on many different levels. While adults will find them meaningful, children will especially appreciate their simplicity and beauty.

These stories of wisdom and compassion can leave a deep and lasting impression on young readers. If children are exposed, on the other hand, to harmful books and confused behavior, much psychological damage can result.

For this reason, Nazli Gellek selected a few tales which could be made available to a wide audience. They are being published in conjunction with the Tibetan Aid Project, and half of the proceeds are being used to assist Tibetan refugees.

Many of the other three hundred *Jataka Tales* will be published in the series in the future. We wish to dedicate these books to the illustrators, writers, and others who helped produce them.

As you and your children read these tales, may their symbolic meanings continue to grow within you.

TARTHANG TULKU

Founder of Dharma Publishing and the Tibetan Aid Project